Katie Goes Camping

by Fran Manushkin

illustrated by Tammie Lyon

PICTURE WINDOW BOOKS

a capstone imprint

Katie Woo is published by Picture Window Books,
A Capstone Imprint
151 Good Counsel Drive, P.O. Box 669
Mankato, Minnesota, MN 56002
www.capstonepub.com

Printed in the United States of America in Stevens Point, Wisconsin.
112013
007883R

Library of Congress Cataloging-in-Publication Data
Manushkin, Fran.
   Katie goes camping / by Fran Manushkin; illustrated by Tammie Lyon.
   p. cm. — (Katie Woo)
   ISBN 978-1-4048-5731-5 (library binding)
   [1. Camping—Fiction. 2. Fear of the dark—Fiction. 3. Friendship—Fiction. 4. Chinese Americans—Fiction.] I. Lyon, Tammie, ill. II. Title.PZ7.M3195Kar 2010
                                                                   2009030612
[E]—dc22

Summary: Katie has a wonderful time camping with her friends Pedro and JoJo, but when it gets dark the shadows make ordinary things seem frightening.

Art Director: Kay Fraser
Graphic Designer: Emily Harris
Production Specialist: Michelle Biedscheid

Photo Credits
Fran Manushkin, pg. 26
Tammie Lyon, pg. 26

Table of Contents

Chapter 1
The Campsite

Katie was going camping.

"I know all about

camping," she told Pedro

and JoJo. "It's so much fun!"

Soon they reached the woods. "First, we put up our tent," said Katie.

"Watch out!" said JoJo.

"It's falling down."

"I can fix it," said Pedro.

"Way to go!" said JoJo.

"Now, let's explore!" Katie said. "I will show you the pond."

"The pond is the other way." JoJo pointed.

"No it's not!" insisted Katie.

Katie ran
down the path,
but soon she was alone. No
Pedro! No JoJo! No pond!

"I am not scared," Katie
said.

She climbed a rock and
looked around. She
saw JoJo and
Pedro coming.

"Boo!" Katie yelled.

JoJo jumped. "Katie, you
scared me!"

"I'm very wild!" Katie
bragged.

"It's raining," Pedro said.

Soon the rain stopped,

and the sun came out.

"Look!" Katie pointed.

"There's a rainbow! Let's

make wishes on it."

Chapter 2
Around the Campfire

Later, Katie's dad made a

campfire, and they cooked

hot dogs and marshmallows.

"Camping is tasty!"

said JoJo.

Soon it was dark.

Stars filled the sky,

and fireflies filled

the grass.

"I'd like to glow at night,"

joked Katie.

"Me too!" said

Pedro. "Then I'd

never get lost."

"I know a ghost story," said Katie's dad. "Once upon a time, there was a bloody finger."

"Stop!" yelled JoJo. "That's scary."

When they were in their
tent, Pedro asked, "Are there
bears around here?"

"I hope not!" said JoJo.

"I hope we see one," said

Katie.

Chapter 3
Spooked!

Soon Pedro and JoJo fell

asleep, but Katie did not.

She was thirsty, so she

tiptoed out of the tent.

Then Pedro woke up.

He was thirsty too, so he

tiptoed out of the tent.

Then JoJo woke up.

"Where is everyone?"

she said. "I don't want to be

alone."

She tiptoed out of the tent.

It was very dark.

"Oh no!" said Katie. "I see

a bear — with antlers."

Katie began running.

Pedro saw something dark.

"It's a ghost!" he yelled.

Pedro began running!

JoJo turned on her

flashlight.

"I don't see a ghost!" She

laughed. "I see Katie and

Pedro chasing each other!"

"I wasn't scared," Katie
insisted.

"And I wasn't!" said
Pedro.

"Oh sure." JoJo laughed.

Back in the tent, JoJo

asked Pedro and Katie,

"What did you wish on the

rainbow?"

"I wished I could see a

ghost," said Pedro.

"You did," said Katie.

"Almost!"

"I wished
to go camping
again," said
JoJo.

"That's an easy wish to get!"
Katie smiled.

"I wished I was a better camper," Katie said.

"You are a great camper!" Pedro laughed. "You are so much fun!"

"My dog likes camping with you too," said JoJo.

"Arf!" JoJo's dog agreed.

Then all the campers fell asleep.

About the Author

Fran Manushkin is the author of many popular picture books, including *How Mama Brought the Spring*; *Baby, Come Out!*; *Latkes and Applesauce: A Hanukkah Story*; and *The Tushy Book*. There is a real Katie Woo — she's Fran's great-niece — but she never gets in half the trouble of the Katie Woo in the books. Fran writes on her beloved Mac computer in New York City, without the help of her two naughty cats, Cookie and Goldy.

About the Illustrator

Tammie Lyon began her love for drawing at a young age while sitting at the kitchen table with her dad. She continued her love of art and eventually attended the Columbus College of Art and Design, where she earned a bachelors degree in fine art. After a brief career as a professional ballet dancer, she decided to devote herself full time to illustration. Today she lives with her husband, Lee, in Cincinnati, Ohio. Her dogs, Gus and Dudley, keep her company as she works in her studio.

Glossary

antlers (ANT-lurz)—large, bony structures on the head of a deer, moose, or elk

bragged (BRAGGD)—talked in a boastful way about how good you are

explore (ek-SPLOR)—to travel in order to discover what a place is like

insisted (in-SIST-id)—demanded very strongly

marshmallows (MARSH-mal-lohz)—soft, spongy white candies

tiptoed (TIP-tohd)—walked very quietly on or as if you were on the tips of your toes

Discussion Questions

1. Have you ever been camping? What did you like best about it?

2. What sort of animals might Katie see in the woods?

3. Do you know any ghost stories? Share one.

Writing Prompts

1. Katie and her friends make a wish on a rainbow. What would you wish for if you saw a rainbow? Write your wish in a complete sentence.

2. Draw a picture of yourself in a tent. Write a sentence that describes how it feels to sleep in a tent.

3. List five things that are useful on a camping trip.

Having Fun
with Katie Woo

In this book, Katie takes a camping trip. When you go camping, you have to pack everything you'll need. Here is a fun game for two or more players that makes you think about what to pack for a camping trip.

The Camping Trip Game

What you do:

1. The first player says, "I'm going on a camping trip, and I am going to bring . . ." Then the player lists something that starts with the letter A, maybe apples.

2. The next player takes his or her turn now. They say, "I'm going on a camping trip, and I'm going to bring . . ." Player two lists something starting with the letter B.

3. The game continues on. Each player takes the next letter in the alphabet.

To make it a little harder, try:

• Using two or more words that start with your letter. For example, if your letter is D, you could bring a dozen donuts.

• Make it into a memory game. Each player has to repeat what the other players have said, going through the alphabet. Try to remember the whole list, right down to the zany zookeeper.

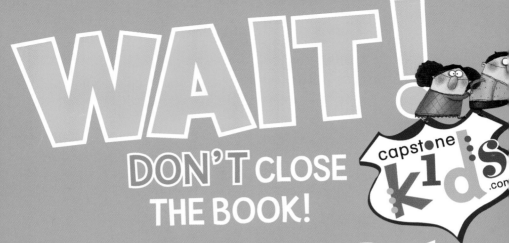